Mr Punch

Bill Ridgway

First published in 2001 by:
Nelson Thornes Ltd
Delta Place
27 Bath Road
CHELTENHAM
GL53 7TH
United Kingdom

01 02 03 04 05 / 10 9 8 7 6 5 4 3 2 1

A catalogue record for this book is available from the British Library.

ISBN 0-7487-6061-X

Cover artwork by Zhenya Matysiak
Typeset by Tech-Set Ltd, Gateshead
Printed and bound in Great Britain by Martins The Printers Ltd, Berwick upon Tweed

1

'Good morning, Mr Wild. What are you doing lying there in the dark? It's a lovely day. I'll just draw the curtains. You'll feel more cheerful with a bit of sunshine in the room. I'll get your wheelchair. You can have a nice chat with your friends. I'll put you by the window where it's nice and warm. You can see the sea from here. Mr Wild – can you hear me? Doctor! Doctor! Mr Wild's having a fit. It was when he looked through the window. I thought the view would do him good. The sea. The people. The Punch and Judy show . . .'

Nurse Bennett rushed Mr Wild into Dr Gliddon's room and left. Mr Wild had stopped shaking, but his eyes were empty and staring.

'I hope you're feeling better now, Mr Wild,' said the doctor. 'We like our patients to be happy in Dreamlands Nursing Home. We thought you were making good progress after your stroke. Nurse Bennett thinks something upset you. What was it?'

Mr Wild's face twitched. He could only make a noise in his throat. Dr Gliddon said, 'I see from your notes you were a policeman, Mr Wild. And you stayed in the police force for over thirty years. Then you had to leave . . . some problems . . . you had a breakdown . . . your wife was killed in a road accident . . .'

Mr Wild's hands were shaking as if he were having an electric shock. Dr Gliddon picked up a pen and some paper. 'Mr Wild, I need to know what upset you. If I draw the thing that upset you, nod your head.'

Dr Gliddon drew a house and turned the paper so Mr Wild could see it. Mr Wild hardly looked at it. Next he drew a boat. Then the sun. Then the cliffs. Mr Wild stared at the drawings, then at Dr Gliddon.

Dr Gliddon looked at the wall, thinking. This time he drew a nose. A huge nose like a hook. He drew two eyes. Evil eyes. A long chin like the moon. He drew an untidy fringe of black hair and a pointed hat.

The doctor forgot about Mr Wild. The figure on the paper was taking shape. A crooked figure with a frilly collar and black boots. 'Mr Punch,' he said to himself.

He turned the drawing so Mr Wild could see it. 'Mr Punch from the Punch and Judy stall. Does he upset you Mr . . . ?'

Tears were running down Mr Wild's cheeks. He was holding his hands to his eyes as if to block out the figure on the paper. Dr Gliddon pressed the buzzer. Nurse Bennett came in. She pushed a needle into Mr Wild's arm.

6

Mr Wild grew still. Then his head fell to one side. Dr Gliddon mopped his brow. 'Strange,' he said. 'It was when I drew Mr Punch. There must be a reason for all this. Put him to bed. And get me the key to his locker.'

2

It was dark and the blinds were drawn. A pool of light shone across Dr Gliddon's desk. It lit up the contents of Mr Wild's locker.

Dr Gliddon picked up a photograph. It must have been Mr Wild's wife. The writing on the back said 'To Ben, Much Love, Nancy'. Dr Gliddon smiled and put it to one side.

There was a penknife. He opened and shut the blades before putting it with the photograph. He took a small box. Inside was a game of moving letters. Dr Gliddon messed with the game for a while and put it with the other things.

He leaned back and yawned. It was nine o'clock. There was only one more thing left to look at. He slid it under the lamp.

It was a thin leather case. The doctor unzipped it and put his hand inside. He pulled out a ring file. He reached into the case again. He took out an old black diary. There was something else too. A cardboard folder. He opened the flap. Cuttings. Old newspaper clippings.

He took out a cutting and rubbed his eyes. The paper was creased and torn. He picked out the words 'Mr Punch Killer Gets Life'. A date had been written in pencil on the cutting.

The cutting was very old.

A shiver went through Dr Gliddon. What was all this about? He had to know. The clue to what had happened to Mr Wild was there on the desk in front of him. He forgot he was tired and pressed the buzzer.

The night nurse came in. She was surprised to see Dr Gliddon still in his office. 'Nurse, I have some important matters to attend to. Could you get me a large coffee, please? And tell the night staff I don't want to be disturbed.'

When she'd gone, Dr Gliddon rang his wife. 'I'll be late back. Something has cropped up.'

He pushed the clips and diary to one side and opened the ring file. It contained some handwritten sheets. It might have been a school file. But for the first page. On the first page were five words:

'THE TRUTH ABOUT MR PUNCH'

3

Mr Gliddon put on his glasses. He opened the file
and began to read.

***

'My name is Matthew Bright. I'm writing this in a cell.
Everyone thinks I did the murders. What a laugh! I
can't even watch a film in case someone gets killed.
They got it all wrong. But they will never believe me.
Who can blame them? It all sounds crazy. I know
that. But it's the truth.

I've decided to write it all down in this file. I'm not
writing in the hope some bigwig will read it and set
me free. To tell you the truth, I'm safer where I am.
I've got my books. And a radio. And the warders are
OK when you get to know them.

No, I'm writing this because I need to set the record
straight. Because – well, if you must know, I don't
think I'll be here long. I don't think I'll be anywhere
long. Death is just around the corner. It could be in
this cell now. Under the bed. Through the window.
He'll get me in the end. I know he will.

But I'm moving too fast. I'd better start at the
beginning.

I always lived by the sea. I was born in a little house by the pier. There's a fair there now, and an amusement arcade. But one thing stayed. The Punch and Judy show. That's still going strong.

I was always drawn to Punch and Judy. As a kid I'd watch the show for hours. There was Mr Punch, with his huge nose and his stick. Then there was his wife Judy and the baby. Sometimes there was a dog called Toby, a clown and a hangman. Even a crocodile and a policeman. It was all down to which show you watched.

The story was nearly always the same. Punch is a psycho. He goes round beating people with his stick. First the baby, then his wife. Sometimes he kills his wife and sometimes he kills other people. Then the hangman comes up and takes him away.

Mr Punch always escapes in the end. I used to be there, looking up at the stall, listening to all those squeaky voices. He was real to me, you see. There was magic in those puppets. I used to be scared and excited at the same time. I forgot there was some bloke behind a curtain. At least, until the end of the show when he came out with his cap. People put money in it. Not much, but with 40 people looking on it was enough to keep him going, I suppose.

I got my Dad to knock me up a stall and I got some puppets from somewhere and pretended to do a Punch and Judy show in my bedroom. I was only a kid. The puppets looked nothing like Punch and Judy but I believed in them. I got really good. I got to do Mr Punch's squeaky voice. I even invented stories of my own.

I grew up. I grew out of a lot of things. I got fed up with toy cars and games and all that sort of stuff. But one thing stayed with me. Punch and Judy. I was as mad on Mr Punch and his crazy world as ever.

That's the reason I'm in a cell writing this. In for murders I never did. But at least I'm safe. For the moment.

4

I left school and went to work as a postman. I liked being on my own. I enjoyed walking. Rain or sun, it made no difference to me. I used to take the mail to the villages in the hills. At first I went by bike. Then they gave me a van.

It was a bright summer's day and I'd finished early. On my way back to the depot I noticed a car boot sale in a field. I had a bit of time so I thought I'd have a look round before I went back.

I was on my way out when something caught my eye. It was a head. A wooden head. There was something about it. It gave you the shudders just looking at it. That ugly, hooked nose. Mad-looking eyes that seemed to stare right into you.

I suddenly realised why I was looking at it. It was Mr Punch. The same eyes, the same nose. I hated it and loved it at first sight. I had to have it.

"How much do you want?" I asked.

"You can have it for £1," said the man. I nodded and he began to wrap it up. "To tell the truth, I'll be glad to get rid of it. That's why I'm letting you have it for £1."

I gave him a coin. He looked as if he wanted to say more. As I turned to go, he said, "You'll find it's slightly scorched down one side. You can hardly tell. You remember Drake Hall got burnt to the ground last year?" I said I did. It was in all the papers. "Well, there was nothing left. I was out walking the dog shortly after it happened and I found the head in the ashes. I took it to the museum. They didn't want it. They said it was probably from a banister or something. So I kept it."

"And you say you're glad to get rid of it?" I reminded him.

"That's right. You know what they said about Drake Hall? It was supposed to be haunted. Everyone round here knew. It may sound daft, but after I took the head home nothing seemed to go right. On the first day, I tripped and fell downstairs from top to bottom. Then my brother got drowned in a boating accident. I shouldn't be telling you all this. The head was carved years ago. It's worth a lot more than £1. I just didn't feel comfortable with it staring at me every night from the shelf. Maybe it's me. You'll probably be fine. But just watch yourself, that's all."

Someone else came up and I left. I got into the van and put the head by me on the seat. On the way back to the depot, the man's words ran through my mind.

14

But I shook myself free of them. It was all a silly story. Just a silly story.

I dropped down the hill. A mist had come off the sea and I suddenly saw two red lights shining through the grey. I stamped on the brake and skidded right into the back of a truck. I hit my head on the windscreen and it shattered. For a moment I must have blanked out.

When I came to, the truck driver was looking in at my window. "Are you all right, mate?" he asked. I nodded. There was a lump the size of an egg over my eye. "You should watch where you're going," he said. "Your van's had it. Hang on and I'll phone for a breakdown truck."

I rubbed my sore head. As I rubbed, I looked down at the seat. The wooden head had broken free of its paper wrapping. The red eyes were staring hard into mine.

Did I imagine it, or was the wide, ugly mouth smiling?

5

The head looked just like Mr Punch. The same huge, hooked nose. The same beady eyes. The same cruel mouth with its rows of sharp teeth. All it needed was a body.

I set to work to make one. Every night I did a little bit. I wasn't very good at first but I got better. I cut out the shape of the chest and the hump back from two pieces of strong cloth. I sewed on the arms and legs to make a body. I cut out some more material. I used red for the coat and white for the big collar. I made boots from shiny black plastic.

I had to do everything myself. There was no one to help. No wife, no girlfriend. Anyway, I didn't want anyone to know what I was doing. They'd think I wasn't all there.

My mates thought I was just someone who worked on the Post. They didn't know I'd always had this obsession with Punch and Judy shows. They thought I'd be working on the Post until I grew old. They were wrong. Buying the head had made me realise what I'd really known all along.

16

I was going to be a Punch and Judy man. I hadn't said a word to anyone. Why should I? But that's what I was going to do. I'd finish Mr Punch. Then I'd make the other puppets. His wife Judy, the baby, the policeman, the crocodile. I'd make a stall and go to the Council to get a permit.

In summer there were thousands of kids on holiday. I'd do Punch and Judy shows to make myself some money. Then I'd get some part-time work on the Post over the winter.

I'd nearly finished Mr Punch. There was only one thing left to do before I joined the body to his head. I had to make a hole in his neck. The hole had to be big enough to take my finger. Then I could make Mr Punch nod. Or shake his head. Or bow. He'd come to life.

I remember thinking, "He'll be more than just a puppet". I didn't know then how right I was. But I should have known. I had a warning. He warned me. Mr Punch.

For as soon as I began to drill the hole a yell blasted my eardrums. The next thing I knew I was slumped by the wall of the garage.

I knew what people would think. They'd think I got a shock from the drill. Getting an electric shock can sometimes do strange things to your body. That's what they'd think.

But how would they explain the look of hate on the face of my puppet? How would they explain the cry of pain that came from the wooden head.

And how would they explain the fact that Mr Punch had bitten the drill in half with those sharp wooden teeth?'

***

6

Dr Gliddon took off his glasses. He rubbed them with a rag. The story he'd been reading lay all over his desk.

He was surprised to find he was sweating. The room was not warm. Droplets of sweat stood on his forehead. He wiped them off and had another sip of coffee.

He went back to Matthew Bright's papers. It was late and the doctor was going to leave it till tomorrow. But he couldn't. He had to know what happened. He picked up the next sheet and carried on reading.

***

'You might think I should have been put off. I wasn't. I began to look on things as a challenge. I worked on the puppets all winter and as soon as I'd finished making them I started on the stall. I looked in books to see how to make it. I used wood and I painted it in bright colours. It had curtains at the top. When they were opened you'd be able to see Punch and Judy and the others.

When I'd finished the stall I practised a show. I could fit inside the stall with no problems. Holding the puppets up made my arms ache at first, but I soon got used to it.

I could still do Mr Punch's squeaky voice. And I thought up other voices for Judy and baby and the hangman and the others. Soon I was thinking up plays for them all to do.

The plays all had one thing in common. Mr Punch always beat his wife. Sometimes he hit the baby too. He beat his wife with a stick. The stick I used in the show was only the same size as a clothes-peg. I had to hold it between my finger and thumb, but to the kids watching Mr Punch would be holding it in his hands. It would be like me holding a club.

I painted the stick black. Usually Mr Punch would murder Judy by beating her with the stick. Sometimes Judy would come back as a ghost and haunt her husband. Sometimes she wouldn't. Whatever happened, he would be taken away by a policeman and locked in a cell. Then along would come the hangman ready to take Mr Punch to the gallows.

Mr Punch would talk himself out of being hung. He was a clever one, Mr Punch. The more I practised, the more I enjoyed the shows. They seemed to take me over. They had a life of their own.

Then one day I was ready to take my Punch and Judy show on the road. The old Punch and Judy man had retired. I got a permit from the Council and set up my stall in a little park by the sea where there were plenty of seats. It was school holidays. By the time the show began there must have been over 100 kids looking up at the curtains.

Now for it. "I'm Mr Punch," I made the puppet say in my squeaky, squeaky voice. "Say hello to Mr Punch." Some children seemed scared. Some said hello back.

Suddenly Mr Punch began to beat the side of the box with his stick. He was screaming out loud. It was me screaming, but I couldn't do anything about it. Me and Mr Punch seemed to be one. It was as if he'd taken me over.

Some of the kids laughed. Some of them just fixed their eyes on evil Mr Punch and didn't even blink. I found myself bringing Judy onto the stage.

"Hello, Judy," Mr Punch squeaked. "Hello, Baby." I felt the little stick in my hand take a swipe at Judy. She fell over and my hand went limp. She didn't move. I couldn't move my hand for a long time.

"Goodbye, Judy," went on Mr Punch. I can't remember much after that till I heard the kids clapping outside. Then I realised the show was over. I must have been through the whole play without knowing it.

I left the puppets in the stall and went outside with an old hat. In five minutes I collected a capful of money. When everyone had gone I packed up the stall and puppets and went back to my flat.

I'd made nearly £30. Not bad for a first show. I began to pack the puppets neatly into a box ready for tomorrow's show. And it was then that I noticed. Mr Punch's little stick had something on it. Something red and sticky.

7

No, I can't explain how blood came to be on the stick.
Puppets don't bleed. Puppets don't die. Puppets
don't have lives, do they?

What are they? Bits of cloth with funny heads.
Squeaky voices and tiny legs. They're nothing on
their own. I made them move. I made them speak. I
made Mr Punch beat Judy with his stick. At least,
that's what I used to think. Now I don't know. I prefer
to leave thinking to other people. Thinking frightens
me. It would frighten anyone who's been through
what I've been through.

I still have bad dreams. Not as bad as before. Then I
used to have nightmares night after night. I'd wake in
a sweat. I'd see Mr Punch's horrible face swimming
out of a red fog. He'd be squeaking in that shrill voice
of his. Screaming with rage. I always woke up just as
he went for his stick.

Sometimes when I woke up I could swear the puppet
wasn't where I'd left him before I went to bed. I
know it wasn't. In the end I shut Mr Punch in a box
and pulled down the lid. The bad dreams still go
on. I still think I can hear him banging, trying to get
out.

But my shows grew more and more popular. Children came from miles around to see them. I started to do two a day, then four, then six. Before summer was out I was making nearly £1,000 a week. A lot of money, and much more than I was making driving a Post van.

Soon the holidays were over and I packed up my stall until next year. And it was then the trouble really began.

I'd put up with bad dreams. I'd put up with the strange things that kept happening. Blood on Mr Punch's stick. The puppet moving by itself at night. All that was nothing compared to what happened next. Because what happened next put me in this cell.

It all began with a local radio programme. I had a lot of time on my hands. I had enough money to last me through the winter and I didn't need to work on the Post part-time. I spent hours listening to music on the radio.

You know those jokey radio DJs. A bit of music, a bit of chat, a few gags. They can keep it going for hours. Well, on this day the DJ broke off playing records to announce the birthday of some girl called Judy in the radio office. He finished by singing "Happy Birthday".

I thought that was that, let's have some more records, when he said, "Are there any more girls out there with the name Judy? If there are, and you can prove to us you were born in the same year and the same month as our Judy, we'll send you a prize. You'll receive a cheque for £20. Each, that is. All you have to do is send in a copy of your birth certificate and you'll get a £20 cheque. No catches. £20 to spend, just for being Judy."

The following day three women phoned in. They chatted with the radio DJ. He made a few jokes like they always do. Then he asked them where they lived.

He should never have done that. If they hadn't told him where they'd lived, they'd still be alive today.

Because I know Mr Punch heard every word.

8

The night the first girl was murdered, I had the worst nightmare ever. I woke up shivering. I had to get up and make myself a cup of tea. I didn't go back to bed that night.

In the morning I went into my bedroom. Mr Punch was still in his box, but there was a stain on the carpet nearby.

It was blood. That's what I'd seen in my nightmare. I'd seen blood on my carpet. And the stain was right by the box. I lifted the lid. Mr Punch was in there with the rest. I took him out. I felt his eyes boring into me. I looked away. Where was his stick?

I found it in the box. It was red. I gave a cry and dropped it. A shrill laugh ran through the room. Or had I imagined it? I dropped the puppet back in the box and shut the lid. Then I put some heavy books on top.

When the paper came an hour later the murder was headline news. 'Radio phone-in girl murdered.' The police said she had been beaten with a blunt instrument.

What a fool I was. Why hadn't I noticed before? Her name. Judy. Punch and Judy. Mr Punch always beat Judy, didn't he? That's what I did in the stall, in my Punch and Judy show. That was not real. That was pretend.

But the headline in front of me was real. The girl was dead. And no matter how crazy it seemed, I knew who the killer was.

How could I tell the police? How could I tell them there were two more Judys who might never see next week? And how could I stop it happening all over again?

9

I just said there were two other Judys. But I was
forgetting the one who worked at the radio station. I
feel crazy when I say Mr Punch knew where to find
them all. Puppets can't know anything. They can't
hear anything. They can't see anything.

That's what I thought. But my Mr Punch was no
ordinary puppet. He might have been made out of
wood and old cloth but he had a life of his own. An
evil life. The devil was inside him, making him do
wicked deeds. Making him kill anyone called Judy.

I didn't know what to do. How could I tell the police?
What could I say? I had a puppet that went round
killing people with a stick the size of a clothes-peg?
They'd lock me away.

Should I phone the radio station and warn them?
They'd think I was a crank. They'd take no notice. Or
worse still, they'd think I murdered the first Judy and
trace the call. Then the police would be along and I'd
end up . . . well, in a cell. Like now.

Yes, I know. I ended up here anyway, so I might as
well have tried to contact the radio people in the first
place. All that's history now. I didn't and that's that.

I settled for a letter. I cut some words out of the paper and glued them to a sheet so no one would be able to trace me from my handwriting. I posted one letter to the radio station and one to each of the other two girls called Judy. Each one said "This is important. Take great care. Someone is out to get you. Don't go out at night. Lock yourself in."

I wasn't very pleased with myself, but what else could I do? For the first time I began to agree with what the man at the car boot sale had said. He wasn't happy with the wooden head in his house. And I wasn't happy with it in my flat. I began to wish I'd stayed with the Post. I was happy driving my little van round the lanes. I was mad to get mixed up in this Punch and Judy game from the start.

I decided the only thing to do was to get rid of the lot. Stall, puppets, Mr Punch. He'd be the first to go. The only thing that stopped me was fear. To tell you the truth, Mr Punch seemed to have a hold over me. It frightened me to even think about getting rid of him. Who knows what he would do to me?

But I couldn't bear it any longer. Before I went to bed that night I had a big glass of whisky to steady my nerves. Then I crept up to the box where I kept the puppets. I was going to throw the lot into the sea.

I lifted the box up and struggled to the door with it. Then I had a shock. One of the puppets fell through the box onto the floor. It was the hangman. I put the box on its side and looked underneath. There was a big hole in the bottom of the box.

Sweat was running down my forehead and dripping off my nose. I lifted the lid.

He'd gone. Mr Punch was no longer in the box. He'd made a hole in the bottom and left the room. Left the house.

There was no way I could stop him.

10

I knew where he was going. Maybe he'd be there already. I panicked. I was shaking all over.

I ran into the hall and picked up the phone book. It was too late to think about what might happen to me now. It was too late to worry about them tracing the call. I had to help the girls. I didn't want another death on my mind.

I found the first Judy's name and address and rang her number. I let the phone ring for a long time. No one answered. Was she out? Or had she already been . . . No, I didn't dare to think about it. Why didn't she have an answer machine? Why had she put herself in danger? How stupid can you get?

In my fright I was blaming her. I kept talking to myself. "Pull yourself together. Relax. Relax." It did no good. My hand was trembling as I rang the second number.

This girl had an answer machine. I left a message. "Get out. Drive to a friend's house. Anything. Just get out!" I was almost beside myself.

Then I grew calm. A feeling of helplessness came over me. I'd done what I could but it hadn't worked. I picked up the phone a third time and slowly dialled the radio station. Would that Judy still be there? It was late. Maybe she'd already left.

I heard the tone. I waited for someone to answer. I seemed to wait hours. Then a voice came down the line. "Hello. This is KO Radio. Can I help you?"

"Who's that?" My voice sounded weak. Weak with fear or relief. I don't know which. "This is Judy – " I didn't catch her second name. I felt as if I'd been given £1,000.

"Are you alone?" I asked. "Who is this?" she cried. I didn't have time to argue. "You don't know me," I said. "I'm ringing to tell you your life is in danger. If you are alone, please leave right away. I repeat, your life is in great danger . . ."

"Get off this line –" she began. Then there was a scream. It was the most horrible scream I've ever heard in my life.

The phone went dead. I held it to my ear. I was frozen with fear. I didn't know what I was doing. Then I heard loud thuds. And a squeaky voice.

"I hate you, Judy . . . I hate you, Judy" over and over again.

I knew I was too late. Slowly, I sank onto a chair. I felt like a man of 90. All I could hear was the ticking of the clock on the wall and that squeaky, squeaky voice echoing in my brain.

I had to get rid of him. I had to kill him. Kill a puppet? Even then the thought made me laugh. But yes. If you like, kill a puppet. Before it found other Judys and started killing again. The only question was – how?'

***

11

Dr Gliddon felt his heart thumping in his chest. The
room where he was reading was dark apart from his
table lamp. He suddenly felt as if he was being
watched. There was not much left to read. He got up
and looked through the curtains. The dark sea made
sad rushing noises. He shivered. Then he went back
to his desk and turned to the next sheet.

***

'I found myself on my bed. I had all my clothes on. I
must have fallen asleep. But something had woken me
up. What was it? I rubbed my eyes. Slowly the fog in
my brain began to clear. I remembered. Those poor
girls. I wished I could go to sleep again and forget.
I'd rather have nightmares every day of my life
than another girl lose her life. But it was no use
hoping.

There it was again, louder. As if a load was being
dragged across the floor. It reminded me of
something. Suddenly I knew what it was.

It was like the noise made by Mr Punch's tiny feet
when I made him cross the stage in my stall. Only
louder. Much louder.

Mr Punch. He was coming back. I was going to see a puppet come into my room, walk by my bed, climb into a box. Don't laugh. I was past laughing. I wasn't crazy. I'm not crazy now. But what was happening was crazy. And what was happening filled me with terror.

What would I see when that door opened? My guts turned to water. I was almost weeping with fright. The footsteps got nearer.

The door creaked. I felt as if I was melting. I watched in horror as the door swung open.

There stood Mr Punch. His back was lit from behind, and his face was a mask hidden in the darkness of my room. But it wasn't the puppet. The kids wouldn't cheer the Mr Punch who stood at the bottom of my bed. Oh no. This Mr Punch was almost as high as the door. And his little stick was bigger than a club. He had it over his shoulder, just like he did when I made him walk across the stall.

I hardly dared to breathe. What would he do? I hardly dared to look at him. I fixed my eyes on his enormous shadow instead. The hooked nose. The bent back. There, on the wall.

And as I watched, something amazing happened. He began to shrink. The shadow shrank to half size, then less. I looked at Mr Punch. He was the size of a puppet again. I saw him – my heart is hammering in my chest as I write this – I saw him get into the box.

Then everything was still. I lay for an hour, maybe longer. I hardly dared to move. I was thinking of a plan. I had to do something. I had to act. I had to get rid of this devil-monster. And I had to do it now.

Hardly knowing what I was doing, I leapt out of bed and switched on the light. I opened the box. Mr Punch lay inside, looking up at me with those hateful red eyes. I had him in my hands within a second. I ran with him out of the room.

In the kitchen there was a food blender. In the cupboard. I flung open the door. Mugs and plates crashed to the ground. I found it. I pulled it out. I kept trying to get the plug in the socket. My nerves were shredded.

And as I found the socket, I saw a movement out of the corner of my eye. It was the puppet. It was sitting up. It was staring at me. It had its stick in its hand. And it was getting bigger.

I heard myself laughing. But I was no longer myself. I think I was mad. In a moment I'd put Mr Punch in the blender and switched on.

36

The blades bit into his face. The glass turned red. I was cheering. Yelling. Dancing. I was making so much noise I didn't hear the door open.

When I came to, the blender had stopped. And there were three policemen with me in the room.

12

That's how I came to be in this cell. Three girls named Judy had been killed that night. When the police were called to their homes they found a lot of blood. And a trail of blood led all the way to my flat.

When the police came the first thing they did was switch off the blender and rescue Mr Punch. They said he might be evidence and took him away in a plastic bag. I could see they thought I was completely mad.

It didn't take the court long to convict me. They gave me a life sentence and there was nothing I could do about it. I've done five years already. I should feel safe. Being in prison is the safest place in the world, people think. But is it?

Where's Mr Punch now? Every time I hear a noise I jump. And the nightmares go on and on. What did the police do with him? I tried to chop him to bits in the kitchen blender. Would he get me for that? He was evil. He was magic. He could go anywhere, do anything, shrink or grow. I'm always thinking about him. Or it. Whatever it is.

I'm writing this at two o'clock in the morning. I'm not supposed to be writing anything. If the police find out they'll rip up everything I've done. It's very quiet in the cell. All the other prisoners are asleep. You can hear a pin drop.

What's that noise? I swear I can hear a noise in the passage outside. There it goes again. Sort of footsteps. Sort of a dragging sound. It's getting closer. It's stopped outside my door. The door is beginning to – '

***

Dr Gliddon had got to the end of Matthew Bright's story. The writing had got more and more untidy. It had stopped in the middle of a sentence. At the end he could hardly read it. He looked at a mark at the bottom of the sheet. It was a faded red mark, like a splash of blood.

The doctor looked at his watch. It was late. All the old people in Dreamlands Nursing Home were in dreamland. But Dr Gliddon didn't feel like sleeping. He felt like a drink. He went over to a cupboard and took out a bottle and a glass. He filled the glass with whisky and gulped it down.

The drink warmed him and he felt better. He felt he had to find out more. How had his patient, Mr Wild, got hold of Matthew Bright's story? Dr Gliddon remembered how Mr Wild had had a fit when he saw the Punch and Judy show through the window. What was the link between Matthew Bright and Ben Wild?

The doctor looked at the other stuff on his desk. The newspaper clippings. The old black diary. He took another gulp of whisky and pulled the clippings into the light.

13

The first clip was from the *Daily Star*. 'Mr Punch killer gets life.' It said, 'Mad killer Matthew Bright was jailed for life yesterday after being convicted of the murder of four women, all with the name of Judy. Matthew Bright was well known to children holidaying in Seaford, who enjoyed his Punch and Judy shows. Mr Justice Harlow said that Matthew Bright was a cold-hearted killer who deserved to be locked away for the rest of his life. He said no woman would be safe if Matthew Bright were ever freed.'

The next clip said, 'Another Judy killing.' It went on: 'Since convicted killer Matthew Bright was locked up, there have been two more Judy killings. Police believe a copy-cat killer is on the loose. They are doing all they can to find this new killer . . .' The clip was dated a year after Matthew Bright was put in prison.

The third clip said, 'End of Mr Punch. PC Ben Wild made a shocking discovery when he checked Matthew Bright's cell yesterday morning. Matthew Bright, better known as Mr Punch, the Judy killer, was found lying dead in a pool of blood. Police are unable to say more at this stage . . .'

There were no other clips. Dr Gliddon opened the diary. The name on the first page told the doctor it belonged to Mr Wild. It was a diary about his days in the police force. Dr Gliddon flicked over the pages. Dates and days rushed by. He stopped at the date when Matthew Bright died in his cell. The doctor was sure he would find the link between Mr Wild and Matthew Bright on that page.

The writing was small and neat. The doctor's eyes were getting tired. It was past midnight. His wife would wonder what he was doing. But he had to finish.

He rubbed his eyes and began to read Mr Wild's diary.

***

'25 May: Convicted killer Matthew Bright taken from Gratton Jail today by police. I question him about other Judy murders. Was he the only killer or did someone else do the dirty work as well? Is he hiding something?

26 May: I carry on with the interview. MB says he is innocent. He will spend tonight in police cells. I will interview him again tomorrow.'

***

The next entry was much longer.

***

'27 May: I find MB's body in morning. I should have been on duty outside his cell last night. I wasn't. I was talking to an old friend instead. I was first to find MB. I should never have left him alone. I took away the papers he had been writing before anyone found out. There was a puppet on the floor, Mr Punch. What was MB doing with the puppet in his cell? There should have been nothing in his cell but MB and a bed. If the boss finds out I wasn't on duty I've lost my chance of promotion. Had to make it look as if MB killed himself. Had to make it look as if it's just happened. Wipe some of the blood onto the wall. They'll think he ran into the wall. Took papers and puppet up to my locker and lock them in. Then sounded the alarm.

I tell the boss I heard nothing. I tell him I was on duty all night. I tell him I kept checking and that MB was OK. I tell boss MB must have done it just before I went into his cell in the morning. Boss believes me. He says he'll have a word with his friends on the newspaper. He says it's clear MB killed himself and he'll get me off the hook. He says he'll deal with it. I must go home for a day's rest. He says if anyone asks, say it was a terrible accident.'

***

So that explained how Mr Wild came to have Matthew Bright's story. But what had happened to Mr Punch? Dr Gliddon turned the pages of Mr Wild's diary.

***

'13 June: I was taken into hospital today. My nerves are shattered. The doctors say I'm having a breakdown. They say it's the shock of finding MB in his cell.

30 September: My wife Nancy died from injuries early this morning. I can't bear to look at her car. I have asked them to take it away.

24 December: It will be a lonely Christmas without Nancy. I've had nothing but bad luck since I brought that puppet into the house. I have made up my mind to destroy it.

25 December, Christmas Day: The only present I want is to get rid of the puppet. I've kept it in a box since MB died. And now I know why he died. And who the real killer was.

Tonight I went out in a boat and tied an iron bar to Mr Punch's head. Then I threw him into the sea. I watched him sink. I feel as if a weight has been lifted off my back. I'll keep MB's story. If someone finds it after I'm dead they'll know the truth.'

***

The following month there was only one entry.

***

'16 January: Had a small stroke yesterday. My doctor says I have to rest. He tells me to give up work. I tell him work keeps me going. I say when the time comes I suppose I'll end up in Dreamlands Nursing Home like all the rest.'

***

Dr Gliddon smiled a thin smile. He leaned back in his seat. Now he knew the whole story . . .

14

Dr Gliddon put everything back in Mr Wild's locker and went home.

He was late getting to work next morning because there had been a lot of rain in the night and the roads were flooded. The weather got worse during the day. He stood at his office window looking out at the grey sea crashing against the sea wall.

Wave after wave came over. No cars were on the sea road. It was flooded. By the afternoon sea water was coming into the grounds of Dreamlands Nursing Home. Now it was up to the doors. The Fire Brigade put sandbags in front of the building.

The old people didn't care. They were warm and comfortable. Mr Wild was asleep in a chair. He'd forgotten all about Mr Punch. He'd forgotten all about his life in the police force.

The time came for Dr Gliddon to go home. He went downstairs. There was a car park under the nursing home. He went down to get his car.

The car park was under water. But it wasn't too bad. He could still get his car out as long as he went now, before things got worse.

He'd just opened his car door when a wave of sea water came over the wall. It drenched Dr Gliddon and threw something hard against his legs. He swore. He thought he'd been hit by a stone.

He looked down at his feet. He stared. He couldn't speak a word. He started to shake. He tried to cry out but nothing came out of his mouth.

There, washed onto the seat of his car, was a head. A wooden head. With two rows of razor-sharp teeth. And an evil smile that made his blood run cold.